Resonance

By: S. D. Nim

Resonance

ISBN: 979-8-9912884-1-5

Published by S. D. Nim
Printed in the USA
First Printing: August 2024

This book is dedicated to all the people in the world who are forgotten, forsaken, misunderstood, and unseen.

CONTENTS

Resonance

Introduction

Welcome to a journey through the intricate landscape of human emotions, where the heart's deepest secrets and most profound feelings are laid bare. This anthology of four short stories invites you to explore the depths of emotions that touch the very core of our existence.

Within these pages, you will encounter characters who navigate the complexities of their inner worlds, each grappling with unique challenges and heartaches. Through their stories, we delve into the raw and often unspoken facets of human experience, uncovering the universal truths that both bind us together and keep us apart.

"Bereft of Me" captures the raw essence of longing, loneliness, and grief. The protagonist's yearning for connection, juxtaposed with her ultimate isolation, paints a stark picture of the emotional desolation that can accompany solitude. Her attempts at kindness and the fleeting connections she forms highlight the fragile nature of human interaction and the profound need for community and empathy.

"Death of a Friendship" poignantly depicts the anguish of losing a deeply cherished bond. The narrative follows a wolfdog and a fox whose initially joyful and playful friendship is ultimately shattered, revealing the fragility of our connections and the profound emptiness that follows the severance of a once-meaningful relationship. The story explores the emotional depth of alienation and betrayal.

In "A Question of Love," Henry grapples with the grief of losing his wife and his lingering doubts about her. As he watches her videotaped messages from before her death, he wrestles with his insecurities and seeks answers to an immense sense of betrayal. The story delves into themes of grief, trust, vengeance, and irreversible consequences.

In "Travelers," the narrative evokes a profound sense of isolation and despair as the protagonist struggles against a relentless snowstorm, feeling detached, disconnected, and lost. This profound loneliness is punctuated by moments of hope, underscoring the depth of detachment and longing for connection.

These four stories together provide a compelling exploration of the human condition, inviting readers to reflect on their own experiences and emotions.

Within the still, dark
Recesses of our minds,
The rhythmic beating
Of our hearts
Echo our deepest yearnings.

Bereft of Me

A crushing weight pressed forcefully down on my chest, robbing me of breath. I struggled to inhale through the pressure and finally gasped myself conscious.

It took much more effort than it should to refill my air-starved lungs.

Lately, this had been happening a lot. I rarely slept through the night anymore. If not the vivid nightmares, this horrible suffocation would gag me awake.

Sweating—despite the fact that the winter chill managed to creep through the window frame and past the drapes—I sat up and took a few deep breaths.

I looked out the window. The sun shone brightly outside, reflecting off of the blindingly white mounds of snow scattered in piles around the parking lot.

Turning my gaze to the clock on the wall, I noticed that it was already eleven a.m. Since I'd woken up about four times during the night, I did not feel rested in spite of the late start to the day.

Sighing heavily, I began my morning routine.

***

After a very late breakfast, I opened the door to my apartment and peered into the hall. My groceries had just been delivered, so I brought them in and put them away.

I was also expecting a package from the Department Store, but it wouldn't arrive until afternoon. To pass the time, I started cleaning. Soon, I heard someone outside my door again.

The package I'd been expecting had finally arrived. As I retrieved it, I glanced down the hallway and noticed that many of my neighbors had decorated their doors with empty Christmas stockings. I thought: *Wouldn't it be nice if they woke up tomorrow and saw a gift inside the stockings?*

Then, excited for my own gift to myself, I brought the package in and opened it. Although it was too cold to wear the three dresses, I'd purchased them on clearance. They'd cost less than ten dollars apiece.

I had enough saved that I could live off it for a few years, but I tended to be frugal anyway because I had decided to take an indefinite break from the remote editing freelance work I'd been doing. I planned to use the next year or two to finally write and publish my first novel.

Smiling about my future plans, I took the dresses out of the box and into my room to try them on. They were all the same size, but the cut made one dress slightly tighter on my bust. I put that one away in a drawer. The next one was too baggy around the waist. Sighing, I placed that one next to the first.

Goldilocks' luck. The third dress fit perfectly, so I put it on a hanger and hung it on a hook on my bedroom door. I planned to wear that dress on New Year's Eve since I had no intention of going out anyway, but I felt like dressing up.

My mind returned to earlier thoughts about the stockings in the hallway. I didn't have a lot of spare money, and I didn't know any of my neighbors personally, but I felt the Christmas spirit and decided to go to the Dollar Store to purchase a few small nicknacks to gift. Maybe they would think Santa really came.

***

Since the parking lot was plowed, the roads must also be clear by now, and today was Christmas Eve. If I wanted to get to the Dollar Store before it closed, I'd have to go soon.

I dressed hurriedly and threw on my coat, but I didn't zip or button it in my rush to get to the store.

I lived in the country, and the Dollar Store was a good half-hour drive from my apartment building. It was already three-thirty p.m. when I set out.

As I pulled my apartment door closed behind me, I looked sadly at the one across from mine. The only neighbors I'd actually met had been Ray and Michael.

They had lived in that now-empty apartment. Since we lived across from each other it had been impossible not to run into each other coming or going, but my other neighbors were spread much farther apart down the long hallway. So, I didn't know any of them.

Ray had observed that I was all alone, so he had made sure to watch out for me. He would often leave a note on my car if he noticed a tire needed air. When he found out my birthdate, he had purchased me a giant card to congratulate me. It was huge, three feet tall and two across.

Michael, his roommate, had offered me a drive to work back when I worked at the bank a few years ago. There had been a terrible ice storm, and my car had gotten stuck on a patch of ice. I could not get it off there without having a tow-truck's help later that day, and my boss said I'd be fired if I didn't make it in. Michael saved my job.

I had really appreciated those neighbors, especially since I didn't have any close friends or relatives.

Some of them, I'd had to cut out of my life because I'd been tired of being mistreated by my loved ones. However, the problem wasn't that I didn't get along with other people; it was just that everyone lived so far away. They were wrapped up in their own lives, so I'd just kind of faded away.

That's what inevitably happened every time. Either people would just forget I was ever there and never contact me again, or they would die.

Like Ray and Michael. Ray had died suddenly several months back due to an overdose. Michael had found him too late to do anything, and he had been devastated. Only two months later, Michael also passed away from pneumonia.

I didn't find out until the landlord came to clear out the apartment, and I happened upon him opening the door.

The memory filled me with profound sadness. So, I rushed to the stairs and hurried to my car, trying to avoid thinking further about it.

***

By the time I got there, it was already dark, and I silently cursed the winter days when the sun was down by 4 p.m. On my way into the Dollar Store, I noticed a strange man leaning against the building. He didn't look in my direction, so I hurried past him into the store.

I don't like to spend a lot of time shopping, so I was in and out fairly quickly. When I came out the man was still there. Only now, he *did* look at me. As I stepped into the semi-well-lit parking lot the icy wind gusted and pushed my shirt tightly against my body, exposing my figure under it fully to the man's view since I still had not fastened my coat.

He leered sinisterly at me—at the curve of my breasts under the shirt. He gave me the impression that he wasn't just content to look, and sure enough he stepped away from the wall. Very frightened, I walked as quickly as possible toward my car without betraying my fear to the man.

Quickly, I thought of a way to trick him. I used my remote starter covertly to turn on the car. It worked. He hesitated, thinking that someone waited for me in the car. He couldn't see into it because the side windows were tinted. I wanted him to believe I was not alone; so I climbed into the passenger's seat and locked the doors.

However, the man did not give up. He walked close to my car on his way to a large, brown pickup truck. It was parked in the row facing where my car was parked, three cars over to my right, and he had a good view of my front window.

He saw me scooting over to the driver's side! He smiled.

I was really afraid, and I tried to get out of there as quickly as possible, but I knew that the man would try to follow me. I didn't want to lead him to my home.

Luckily, I remembered that there was a Rental Moving center close by where I could lose him. The Rental Moving center was in the opposite direction from my apartment. So I turned left out of the store parking lot instead of right. But I had only thought of it as I neared the turn, so I had to switch lanes. I saw the pickup truck in my rearview mirror. He switched lanes after me. He *was* following me, and he was too close to lose easily!

I drove down the street and took the turn into the dirt driveway for the Rental Moving center. The driveway was almost impossible to see in the dark, and I would have missed it if I hadn't known it was there. I followed the driveway to the right and drove past the front of the Rental Moving service trailer.

There were no lights anywhere nearby to illuminate the area. I thought about using my cell phone to call the police, but I knew there wouldn't be any time for that. He had followed me into the driveway! What's more, when he saw how dark it was, he'd turned off his headlights.

There were no signs or Rental Moving trucks near the trailer now. He must have thought I lived in the trailer. I couldn't stop or hesitate. I had a plan to escape, and I had to use it. The driveway was very narrow and hard to get out of once you pulled in, but I knew that I could circle behind the trailer and get back to the driveway entrance and out again.

I turned left and left again, quickly going around and behind the trailer. The land there was a hill and very uneven. I went over a boulder that protruded slightly from the ground, and the car jostled severely, slowing me down. I hit the gas to get the car moving faster. I could not afford to lose any time!

Because the man had turned off his headlights, he couldn't see where I'd gone after I curved around the trailer. I drove past the other side of the trailer and back out behind the man's truck. I got onto the road and turned in the direction of my apartment.

I'd lost him.

Still, I was afraid to go directly home. I drove past the turn to my apartment complex and stopped at the brightly lit gas station down the road.

I looked around for several minutes from my parked, locked car. I thought about calling the police, but the town I live in doesn't have a police force of its own. The state police would have taken a long time to get there, and I figured they wouldn't be able to do anything now anyway. Also, I couldn't really describe the man physically. I'd been too scared to stop and really look at him, and a lot of people drive pickup trucks in the country.

Several minutes passed as I sat there, my heart pounding. Then, I felt a fluttering sensation in my chest. My vision began to darken as my body seemed to lose all strength.

Frightened, I inhaled deeply. My heartbeat returned to normal, and my vision cleared up again.

The man never reappeared, so I finally headed home.

***

As I sat on my couch wrapping the little figurines and snow globes I'd gotten, my hands still shook involuntarily from the ordeal.

I took one of the candy canes I'd purchased to hook into each stocking and started eating it to distract myself.

As I continued wrapping, I suddenly heard someone start to bawl uncontrollably. The person seemed to be sitting on the stairwell next to my apartment because I could hear it very clearly.

After several minutes had passed, I took a break and went to make myself a quick dinner. Yet, even after cooking and eating the person still persisted in crying her heart out.

I felt so bad for her, even though I didn't personally know who it was or why she could be crying in such a heart-wrenching manner for so long.

I began thinking that she surely must be very thirsty by now, and she must need a tissue.

So, uncharacteristically, I decided to go out to the stairway and meet the sad stranger. I took the last bottle of water I had and some tissues out to her.

I felt terrible because she seemed so startled by me.

"I'm really sorry. I heard you crying, and I thought you could use these," I explained awkwardly as I handed the items to her.

Her expression showed neither relief nor gratitude for the proffered items. Instead, she looked mortified. Deeply embarrassed, she accepted them with shaking hands.

Maybe I had inadvertently taken away her safe space, where she'd thought she could let it all out without anyone knowing.

I did my best to set her at ease with a gentle smile and finished by saying, "If you need anything, I live in apartment 15B, there in the corner."

Yet as I saw the woman's reaction, I felt certain that I'd never see her again. Self-consciously, I hurried back into my apartment, not wanting to make her feel any worse. I heard the woman running from the stairwell as soon as I left. Not knowing if I'd done the right thing, I returned to wrapping.

Looking at the little pile of gifts, I suddenly got the idea that I should wrap up my dresses as well, so I'd also have something to open tomorrow morning. I still had a bunch of boxes from past deliveries that needed to be recycled at the end of the week. So, I got the two dresses from the drawer and put each into its own box. I wrapped them up beautifully.

Finally, I finished. Now, the only thing left to do was to deliver the small gifts to their stockings in the wee hours of the morning, when I was sure everyone had gone to sleep. I sighed deeply, thinking about what had happened after I'd left the store. It made me shudder.

At that moment I felt a sudden pressure in my chest. Once again, the palpitations resumed, and I wondered if they were caused by stress. Only this time, they didn't stop after a few seconds or even after a minute.

I felt breathless, my chest tightening as everything began to go dim. I slumped back on the couch, clutching my chest as consciousness began to quickly slip away. I didn't have the strength or breath to call for help.

If I died here, now, no one would miss me. Not even the debt collectors would notice if I disappeared. Everything was on autopay.

Desperately, I tried to reach for my phone, but my arm just felt so heavy.

I couldn't help but think: *I'm scared. I don't want to die all alone in the dark.*

The intensity of the discomfort in my chest worsened. Rather than a heartbeat, there persisted a violent trembling. Everything suddenly went black.

*The past cannot be changed,
but we still have the present.*

The Death of a Friendship

Once there lived a creature who was half wolf, half dog.

The dog side of him made him playful, friendly, and adventurous. The wolf side of him was also sociable, but selective. It made him yearn for a place where he belonged.

Because of his wolf blood, the wolfdog was not trusted by man, who usually adopted friendly, playful puppies and built life-long friendships with them.

His wolf family had also rejected him due to his mixed blood, but his mother had managed to flee the pack with him to save his life after the new alpha had killed all her other pups.

***

The wolfdog grew up into a healthy, young animal and spent his days exploring the world. He befriended stray dogs and some other curious animals he met along the way.

However, he avoided following dogs to towns or villages where people lived because he knew there would be danger there. So, he rarely saw his dog friends.

That left the other animals he knew. With those, he maintained more reserved friendships based more on curiosity than anything else.

There were the birds who lived by the babbling brook. They sang beautiful songs that pleased the wolfdog very much. They enjoyed receiving his praise and sang for him regularly but kept their distance.

The snapping turtle that hunted fish in the brook would sometimes leave some uneaten portion for the wolfdog. Still, if the wolfdog got too close, the turtle would snap at him harshly.

Then, there was the fox.

***

The fox had also been ostracized by her family at a young age because, in the animal world, if one is born with a defect, that animal is killed immediately.

The day her mother had decided to end the little fox, a human being had happened to stumble across their den.

The woman had seen the fox mother entering with some food, and the fox mother had seen the woman almost at the same instant.

Filled with intense fear and the instinct to defend her offspring, the fox mother had forgotten about dispatching the little defective fox.

When the woman finally left, the mother fox took the other pups away at once, abandoning the one little fox there to be discovered by the person when she returned later to get a closer look at the den.

***

In fact, the woman had intended not to disturb the family further. She only walked by the spot to reach a place where she went to pick berries. However, she finally decided to look into the den because she heard the baby fox crying pitifully for quite a long time.

Realizing it had been abandoned, the woman took the pup and cared for it, but she respected the fact that the fox was a wild animal. So the fox had been raised by the woman and then released once she was old enough to fend for herself.

***

In her time at the woman's farm, the fox had seen dogs, cats, and other farm animals. However, she had been kept away from them, able to smell and see them from the other side of a fence, but nothing more.

The dogs would, at times, bark to her, and a few times asked her to come out and play. Though their games looked like fun, the fox had an inherent fear of dogs.

She never ventured near one until she met the wolfdog.

***

Shortly after being released, the fox happened across the wolfdog playing with some of his dog friends. She watched them play with a pink ball, flinging it with their jaws and racing to retrieve it first.

The wolfdog got there first every time. Then, the other dogs finally left, tired. They returned to the town and left the wolfdog there with his ball.

He picked up the ball and turned to see the fox watching him. Dropping it, he said, "What a pretty creature you are! I like your tail."

He went over to sniff her instinctively, as if she were another dog.

"You don't smell like the other dogs," he mused.

"I'm *not* a dog," she replied.

The fox sniffed the wolfdog as well, for some reason not feeling any fear or desire to escape. She somehow felt safe with him.

"Want to play?" he inquired.

The wolfdog took the ball excitedly and threw it to the fox.

"Yes!" she replied, enthusiastically.

The game had looked like a lot of fun. The fox had watched all this time hoping that the dogs would eventually tire and abandon the ball so she could play with it.

Finally, she had the chance.

***

So the wolfdog and fox became friends.

He often invited her to play, even including her when he'd play with other dogs.

If any of the dogs looked at the fox sideways, he'd be there to watch out for her. He really enjoyed her company and had fun playing, particularly when they played ball together. She actually offered decent competition when they'd race after it, unlike his dog friends.

Only the wolfdog still harbored inside him an intense desire that had never been fulfilled. His wolf half called insistently from within.

***

One night, when the moon shone brightly in the sky, he heard wolves howling and couldn't contain his own response in kind. That night he met *her*.

The female wolf was everything he'd ever dreamt of. Not only was she lovely and confident, but she was the alpha of her pack. She had gone to investigate the unknown howl and found him.

Smitten, she'd immediately initiated play and been delighted when the wolfdog followed her.

The other wolves had, at first, been wary of him and sometimes tried to test him to see if he'd back down. Yet, the female alpha and the wolfdog were fierce, especially together.

The wolfdog felt like he had finally found what he was missing. He went off with the female wolf and forgot about his other friends.

***

The fox had gone looking for the wolfdog one day and discovered that he had gone away to join a pack. She hid in the shadows and followed to see what was happening with him.

Though the fox missed the wolfdog, she saw that he was the happiest she'd ever seen him. As his friend, she rejoiced for his happiness.

At one point she had tried to greet him and come face-to-face with the female alpha. Although the wolfdog had come over and greeted the fox as a friend, the female wolf had placed herself between them aggressively.

"This animal is no wolf. She is no friend," said the female wolf.

The fox had fled at that time, but she'd continued to watch the wolfdog from the shadows.

***

The wolf part of him was ecstatic to be in a pack at last. Yet, the dog part of him longed for the freedom he'd once had to explore and play with different animals.

For as a wolf, he was only allowed to associate with the pack. Other creatures were seen as only prey, including other dogs.

The wolfdog was never alone anymore. If he tried to approach a dog or other animal, the pack was there, ready to hunt.

So the wolfdog's perspective changed. He stopped trying to befriend other animals. They became only prey to him.

Except he had not forgotten the fox.

***

On the day the fox ran into the wolfdog alone again, he did not call for the pack to come running. Instead, he quietly slipped away to talk to her.

"How have you been?" she asked, expecting him to tell her of the fulfillment and happiness he felt at last.

It had not escaped the fox's keen observation when they would play together in the past that the wolfdog was often sad and preoccupied.

Even though he had made all the difference in her life, she had not been able to inspire the same joy in him. For what she'd wanted most, she'd found. She had stopped feeling lonely and afraid when they'd become friends.

But the only thing that satisfied the wolfdog was finally being part of his pack.

Still, the wolfdog did not reply as expected.

"I miss you," he said. "I wish we could play with the ball like old times."

This made the fox very happy.

"I still have it. Do you want me to get it?" she asked.

"Now's not a good time. I have to get back. I will see you soon," he said and left abruptly.

***

The joyful fox thought that perhaps the wolfdog would come back the next day. She retrieved the ball that morning and took it to wait where she had seen him.

He did not return.

Each day after, she waited for a while at the spot where they'd met. When the sun set, she took the ball back to her den and went to sleep or went out to hunt.

The wolfdog returned to the pack and continued his life as usual. He had meant to keep his promise to meet the fox, but after a few days passed he forgot about it.

***

A month elapsed, but the fox still went to wait at the spot. She had been busy one day, so she arrived later than usual and fell asleep with the ball next to her.

That night a full moon shone on the fox before she finally awoke. Startled that she had fallen asleep out in the open, the fox picked up the ball and turned to run to her den.

However, a familiar scent on the wind caught her attention. Instead of running back home, the fox turned again and ran toward him.

The wolfdog was hunting with his pack. Since the wind was blowing away from him, he did not smell the fox. However, the bright moonlight revealed her silhouette running in his direction.

He ran toward her, excitement growing inside him. He didn't know what had caused this lucky circumstance, but he was not one to waste an opportunity.

As they ran, the moon hid itself behind a cloud, plunging them into darkness.

The only thing the fox saw were the red glowing eyes of the wolfdog just before he leapt at her and seized her throat in his powerful jaw.

This caused the fox to bite down on the ball in her mouth, locking it there as fangs pierced her tender throat.

It was in that moment that the fox's weak, defective heart finally ceased to function. The valve burst, flooding her insides.

The wolfdog clenched his jaw down tightly until he heard a crack.

The fox had gone completely limp.

Satisfied he'd done his job well, the wolfdog dropped her body to the ground.

At that moment, two things happened at once. The moon revealed itself again, shedding light on the grim scene; the wind changed direction, flooding the wolfdog's nostrils with the fox's scent mixed with death. The wolfdog's eyes widened in recognition.

The fox's eyes were open and saturated with unshed tears. Blood trickled out of the corner of her mouth and pooled by her jaw. The ball remained firmly between her teeth.

*Our connections
extend beyond our perception
into the shared depths
of our emotions.*

A Question of Love

It's nearly 8 p.m., and she isn't home yet. It's okay. I know where she is anyway. I came home early to see her before she went, but she was already gone.

So instead, I invited my neighbor George to come over and play some cards. He's been here for two hours talking on and on about how much his wife nags him. I'm about ready to throw his ass out.

Then I hear someone knocking boldly on the door. I know it isn't her. Even if she'd forgotten her keys, the knock is an authoritative one—the knock of …

I open the door and there is a police officer standing there. I have a moment of panic, but I keep it under control.

"Mr. Brown?" the officer asks, while looking at a notepad.

"Yes," I answer, my legs becoming a little unsteady. Still, I manage to keep my balance, even as the world begins to wobble and turn in my head.

"I'm really sorry to have to tell you this, but your wife …"

I can barely hear as he finishes telling me she's dead. Died in a car accident. It was a fast death; surely, she felt no pain. Dead on impact. Surely. But the words are not comforting, and I collapse finally, overcome by conflicting emotions.

***

The funeral is packed, mostly with her relatives. My family comes briefly to show me their support. They never really liked *her* much anyway. I know now that they may have had a reason not to, but when I met her, fell in love, and married her, I couldn't have understood.

She looks like she's only asleep. They did a really good job covering up her wounds. You'd never know she'd been in a horrible accident. I feel a great sense of loss looking at her face. But then I felt that loss long before today. I still remember the day the detective came to my door. That authoritative knock …

"Henry, are you alright? Maybe you should sit down. I can't imagine how much pain you must be feeling right now…. I'm so sorry for your loss."

It's George's wife, Edna from next door. The nagging woman. She's a good ten years older than I am, as is George. Somehow her face seems to show the age much more when she grimaces like that. I don't want to talk to Edna. I just nod and walk away.

***

I've never been much of a drinking man. I hate the way people act like fools when they are drunk. But somehow, I find myself taking another drink anyway. It tastes like crap, even after the first three. I'm already drunk off my ass, but still haven't reached that fabled numb feeling alcohol is supposed to bring. Dizziness, nausea, thirst, are all I feel. I guess my skin *is* kind of numb, but my feelings are sharp as ever.

I hear a thumping in my head, and it aches at the sound. I'm so groggy. Is that a real sound, or can I actually hear my headache? This is the last time I drink to drown out my sorrow.

But the sound is at the door. Knocking, but not authoritative this time. I stagger over and open it. The too-bright sunlight nearly blinds me and casts the man at the door in silhouette.

"Mr. Brown?"

"Yes?

"Henry Brown?"

"Yes …?"

"I'm very sorry to bother you at home. I've been trying to reach you for the last week. I've sent letters, and tried calling …"

He looks unsurely at the pile of mail tumbling out of the mailbox onto the floor of the porch. Then he stares past me at the phone, its line hanging loose under the desk, obviously not connected to the wall. I see him begin to make an annoyed face, but he recovers quickly.

"I'm very sorry about your loss. I know it must be very difficult for you right now. I knew your wife," he says, and suddenly my blood begins to boil, and I come instantly sober. He continues, "She was a beautiful person …"

"Why are you here? Who are you?" I ask angrily.

The only thing allowing me to keep control is the absurdity of what I'm thinking. Surely, *he* wouldn't come here. He wouldn't have the nerve to come to me to share my grief. Not when everything was *his* fault.

"Oh, I'm so sorry. Of course, I haven't introduced myself."

He seems genuinely perturbed by the omission. Then, he straightens himself and tells me his name. I barely hear it, waiting for the explanation—the real introduction. I want to know why he's here.

"I was Mrs. Brown's lover."

I am shaken to my core. I *must* not have heard correctly.

"You were ..."

"Mrs. Brown's lawyer," he reiterates. "Yes. You see, she had left some things ..."

The vertigo is back. He was her *lawyer*. He has some things he needs to give me, things she left.

He hands me a box and has me sign some paper. Then he apologizes again and tells me that I will need to call in order to set up the reading of the will and settlement of her estate.

I never even knew she had a lawyer. How many other things had she kept secret from me? I'm relieved when he hands me his card and takes off to his car by the curb. He seems relieved too, judging by how fast he climbs into his car and drives away.

***

The large box is made of some kind of plastic. One of those fire-safe safes. The keys are in an envelope taped to the top of the box. It's labeled "Mr. Henry Brown."

I recognize her handwriting and feel a pang in my heart. I try not to cry, but I can't hold the tears back. It's been a week since the *lawyer* dropped off the box. I haven't bothered to call him back. But I can't take it anymore. I need to know what she left me. I rip the envelope open, breaking the blurry name. I unlock the box.

She left me a bunch of CDs. I take one out and examine it. No. It's a DVD. There are twenty DVDs in the box. The first one is labeled "1997." The year we were happily married. What are these? Some old home movies I forgot about? There's one for every year of marriage. The last one is labeled with this year, a neat, black-markered "2017."

I'm tempted to view that one first, but then I can't bear the thought of remembering her the way she was just a few short weeks ago…. Wait…. Has it really been more than a month?

Her image is too fresh in my mind, overlaid with the image of her lying in her coffin. Today, the young woman of 1997 seems far away and dream-like. Better to start there, at the beginning. Maybe I can glean something from the progression of the past into the present. Maybe I will see what led to such a tragic ending and finally understand.

***

I can't understand what I am seeing. It's my wife at 26, sitting in a room. She's talking to me. She's talking to *me!* Now. The me sitting in front of the tv. The me who must be so heart-broken now that she's gone. But she isn't gone. She will never leave me. She's caring for me even now from wherever she is, even though I can't see her.

I pause the DVD. I rewind it.

"Hi Henry. If you are watching this video, it means that I must have died before you. I'm really sorry I had to leave you. I never would if I had a choice. But I never really will. I know how much you love me. I love you so much, and I wouldn't be able to handle it if anything happened to you. That's why I'm making this video. Now that we're married, I want to be sure, that if I died first, you would be okay. You must know that I'm still with you. I will always stay with you, even after I die. Even if you can't see me or hug me anymore. I will stay with you until you die, but I want you to be happy because I'm still here. Really."

***

What a morbid thing to do. She made a video every year to give me more time with her. To get me used to the idea that her spirit will never leave me. To *comfort* me. It would never have occurred to me to do such a thing. But it really is like she's here in the room with me, saying things I never heard her say to me before. It's like she's come back to be with me, to help me not to grieve so hard. But she's young again. So young and remote. I'm afraid to see what will happen over the years. I don't know what she'll be saying when she's 46 again, and telling me what she won't know is her final goodbye.

***

Anxiously, I view DVD after DVD. The hours pass so quickly I feel like the man in *The Time Machine* when the sunsets and sunrises appear and disappear around him at an alarming rate. I barely take time to eat or use the bathroom. I must know why. I must watch the progression.

Then, about the fifth year my wife changes the routine of the DVDs. She says that she has already said a great deal about her beliefs and her feelings about death, but that she wants me to know how she's feeling all along. So she tells me about things that happened that year. Some of them I remember vividly, some not at all. It's always been that way with us. She would hold on to the smallest, simplest memory and attach all kinds of importance to it.

In life it would often cause fights between us, but in death she has chosen to focus solely on good memories and feelings. Memories and feelings involving me. She wanted me to know how important I was in her life, moment to moment.

***

I've reached the 2014 DVD. There has been another change in format. Up until now she has always stayed in one room and narrated to me. Now she has decided to bring some joy back into my life, some new experiences with me. She's taken the camera out with her, sometimes to point it out at the world of 2014, saying things like: "I wonder in 20 years if this will still be the same?"

She took a tour through the park across town. Ironically, only three years later the park is gone, replaced by a parking lot.

In the video, she finds a nice, scenic place and sets up the camera. She looks so vital, so beautiful. She holds up a basket and says, "We didn't really have a lot of time to have picnics so far, and I figure you must not be eating so well since you've been depressed. Although I hope by now you've cheered up some, knowing I'm right here with you. I wish I could kiss you and hug you. I know how important it is to feel that kind of physical presence. But I'll settle for you going right now and getting something to eat so we can share a nice picnic together."

I pause the DVD and do as she wished. I don't feel hungry, and I do feel depressed, but this, in 2014, was still my loving wife. And I could never deny her anything.

***

After the 2014 DVD comes to a close, I hesitate on the 2015 one. That was the year I decided that I needed to work more in order to afford our move into the house I am sitting in right now.

She was very patient with me that year, but I know she was depressed a lot by not being able to spend as much time with me. Then it occurs to me. Could that be the answer? Could that be why she did what she did? But if she really loved me so much, why didn't she talk to me about it? Instead of ... betraying me like that.

Yes, it was in 2015 that I started to suspect something wasn't right between us anymore. But at that time I still hadn't thought what it could be. Would this DVD outline her fall from loving wife to ... I have to know.

***

After viewing it, I reflect on what I noticed. The 2015 DVD did have a difference to it, but it wasn't what I expected. Instead of bitterness and accusation, instead of the purging I imagined she'd take on camera to the me that she didn't really have to face, she was almost desperately the opposite. I could see that she was suffering, but on screen she was comforting herself, as well as trying to comfort me through the suffering.

She said that I'd been gone more often and that I'd been a bit short and grumpy lately, but that she knew I didn't mean it because I'd always been such a loving, sweet man. So she would let it slide. She winked at me.

"This year, I'm going to do something different."

This statement often prefaced a change in the way the DVD would go. She had decided that since we couldn't spend the time together in her present, she would spend it with me in this future.

She knew that I would often miss her and wonder how she spent her day, so she recorded a few minutes here and there of that.

I really enjoyed it when she took me into the kitchen and set up her own cooking show.

It was her way of making sure I learned how to make something on my own so I wouldn't starve to death without her cooking.

But that brings back the fact that she's dead, and also that the next DVD is only a year away from that sudden end.

***

My hand shakes as I take the 2016 DVD and place it into the player. The 2015 DVD left me with the same feeling as the rest. I can't fathom what had led her to do what she did. Based on these DVDs she still loved me as much as ever, and I can't believe she'd taken a lover before 2016.

Last year, I had discovered that she had been taking some time away from work. She would often get home later than I would and be surprised to see me home. I had been working more than ever in the beginning of the year, but once we'd moved into our new house and gotten adjusted, I had seen that it wouldn't actually be necessary to work as long every day as I'd originally thought. I received a great promotion at work and a bonus on top of that. I was thrilled. I wanted to share it with her.

So then was when I noticed how often she would be out during the day, when I'd call to invite her to lunch. I saw how she reacted when I told her I'd planned a vacation for us as a surprise. She seemed more startled than pleased. Somehow, she'd managed to use up most of her vacation days and would need to ask permission for unpaid leave in order to go. When I asked her what she'd done with her vacation days she answered with a cryptic "quality time."

Quality time alone? Had she been so depressed that she'd taken the days off to stay home and cry? No. She'd hardly been home. It was then that I'd decided to find out just where and when she'd been spending this "quality time," and more importantly, with who?

***

I shove the 2016 DVD into the player and watch intently. I want to know the exact moment she changed toward me.

"Hi again, my love. I know I used to start the DVD closer to the end of the year before, but I really have been missing you still. So I couldn't wait. Well since in the last DVD I thought it would be a good idea to share moments now and then in the present—and right now you are working really hard to afford our new house—I thought it would be really nice to share the first tour through it with you after it was finally ours. The moving men have just finished moving everything in, and I took the day off to get it all ready for you."

I remember that day vividly. I had worked past midnight that night and gotten home exhausted and just wanting to fall into bed and sleep. She'd been waiting for me on the couch in our new living room. She'd been asleep when I arrived but was up and hopping around like a schoolgirl when I walked through the door. She had gotten all the furniture set up and had been waiting for me in order to show off what a good job she'd done with it while I was working.

But I was too tired, and I refused to "tour" the house with her that night. I'd staggered up to bed and left her at the bottom of the stairs with a sad-puppy look on her face.

On the DVD, she goes step-by-step arranging little details to make the place homier. She explains how she got the new throw rug for the living room as a surprise for me and is dying to see what I think of it.

She had remembered that I had admired a similar rug at my boss's house when we'd been invited to dinner right before my promotion. At this time in the DVD, the promotion hadn't actually taken place yet.

She went on in that vein for a while, adding romantic touches and details she thought I'd enjoy.

"I know this will already be really familiar by the time you see this. Well maybe you'll be old and gray and long since have forgotten." She laughed.

I keep watching and some of my questions are answered in front of my eyes. She'd taken a vacation day to take me along to the opening of a new museum. I remember that she'd hinted about wanting to see it with me and attend the benefit dinner afterward.

"Forgive me if I tell people I'm recording it for posterity. I don't want them to think I'm morbid." She winked at me. "I'm so happy I can still share this with you though. It's probably more interesting to you in the future anyway.'' She laughed again.

I look for resentment, sarcasm, or malice in the joke and find none. She was in earnest.

And she was right. Back then, I'd been on the verge of getting promoted, but I couldn't have enjoyed myself at the event while worrying about my job. Yet, they wouldn't have postponed the event so that I could attend. She'd saved it for me, for when she thought it would help me to feel better.

***

The DVD is coming to a close. She tells me how much she loves me and how happy she is about the promotion and how she felt a little bad because she hadn't known and had used so many vacation days for the future and made things a little tougher in the present. But she is always glad to spend time with me whenever that may be, and she enjoys the present moments as much as the future moments. Next time though, she'll find time for the DVD that doesn't take time away from what could still be done in her present.

***

I reach the last DVD. 2017. A horrible thought crosses my mind as I put it into the DVD player. The implications are too much to bear.

In early 2017 the detective had come back to me with definitive proof of my wife's infidelity. He had recorded her talking to *him* through the door of a hotel room. She'd told the man how much she loved him and that she would always be with him no matter what, even if she died …

At the time, I had been too shocked to believe what I'd heard. Later, I'd become angry. I'd found myself plotting revenge. I wanted to expose her and throw her out of my life, but I couldn't. Instead I controlled my emotions and became the best husband I could be.

***

The DVD starts with her telling me that she would still be sharing moments from here and there, but that I was around a lot more, so this year would be a year of snippets more than the last year. But not to worry, she is still with me. For the rest of her life she'll be with me, and beyond.

It's like she said. Stolen moments here and there. More and more about how wonderful I was being now that I'd gotten my promotion and we'd been living in our house for a while. She described to me how we were spending more time together and what she felt at those times. She was glowing.

"I love you so much. I'm so happy to spend time with you. I'll always be with you no matter what, even if I die. Remember that. Any moment I can share with you I will be there, even as a spirit."

I stop the DVD. She's in a hotel room, where she'd stayed on a business trip. It's the same. Those words have been etched into my brain from the first time I heard them on the detective's recording.

***

The detective had arrived at my office and knocked his authoritative ex-cop knock. He'd handed me an envelope as soon as he'd walked through the door.

"I've finally got her. The proof you wanted."

At the time, it didn't occur to me to ask about *him,* the man she was cheating with. It was enough to hear her uttering those words to someone else. She'd never been so adamant about saying "I love you" to me. Even after her death she'd stay with *him,* whoever *he* was. I felt betrayed. I felt disgusted and angry. I'd paid the detective and told him to leave. I didn't want to know any more.

Later, I'd read the report and noticed that it was strange that they were never able to get the guy's voice responding to her proclamation, and that they never actually saw him. She could have been talking to him on the phone, but how had they never caught him? It made it worse in my eyes. The man was using her, sneaking away under cover after their liaisons. Maybe he'd even made the detective and his crew. Maybe he was used to boning other men's wives and stealing their love.

***

Now I know how preposterous that sounds. Why couldn't I just have confronted her with my fears? Instead I'd gone to her and pretended not to know. I'd taken my time planning the moment of truth.

I have to see it through to the end. I press play.

More stolen moments and then, suddenly, there is a change. She says she feels weird. She is still really happy, and she can't believe how sweet I'd gotten. She worries that I felt guilty because of working so much the year before. She describes all the things I'd done to surprise her. She thought I'd done them to hide my guilt.

I remember her trying to comfort me and saying that I didn't have to, but at the same time being happy that I'd been so thoughtful. Back then, I'd assumed *she'd* felt guilty about being unfaithful, and that was why she said those things. All along she'd been worried about *me*.

She starts showing a suppressed fear on the screen, and I think for a moment that she had figured out what I really hid behind all those sweet acts, until at last she speaks of her fear.

"Oh Henry. I'm scared. I don't want to leave you. I want to stay with you. I'm only 46, but for several days now I've been feeling a foreboding. You know I sometimes get premonitions of bad things that come true…. I feel like I'm going to die soon. And I don't want to leave you. I had such a bad dream…." She starts crying.

The screen flicks black for a second. Then, suddenly she is there again, and she is fine. She smiles.

"I'm so sorry about that little bit of drama a minute ago. I had a really stupid bad dream, and I got carried away. This isn't what I wanted to leave you with …" She hesitates. Some part of her still feels that the conclusion of the DVDs isn't so far in the future as she'd originally thought.

"You always did hate it when I'd have a bad dream and then take it out on you. Well I wasn't really taking them out on you at the time, just trying to show you that they disturbed me and why. But I won't do that now. The fact is, I have nothing to be scared about. I have nothing to be sad about. We'll have lots more time together. I'll always stay with you no matter what. Even when I die, my spirit will stay with you and try to comfort you. I love you, Henry."

***

That was the end. I sit back against the couch. I've been sitting on the throw rug she'd gotten me as a surprise, the surprise I only just discovered in the videos. She gave me 20 years, and eternity if the DVDs are to be believed.

Is it possible she will really stay with me forever, loving me—the man who paid to have her killed in an "accident?"

Travelers

One cold winter's night, I found myself walking through a terrible snowstorm. I struggled in the blinding, wind-swept snow to find my way to some sort of shelter. I could not see where I was going. I could only feel the biting cold of the wind and the wet snow.

Finally, I collapsed near a tree. I do not know where the tree came from. It seemed to appear there, next to me. It blocked a great deal of the wind and snow, which was coming down at an angle on the other side of the tree.

Freezing, exhausted, I lay there by the tree and rested. The snow swirled frantically through the air, obscuring the moonlight. I could not see in the dark.

Every part of me integrated itself with the frozen terrain. My stiff limbs were like the branches of the tree. My breath added itself to the chilled wind, blowing snow gently into swirls in front of me. I felt detached from my body. I could not feel my heart beating in my chest.

When the wind began to calm, and the snow slowed and ceased to block out the soft glow of the moon, I looked up and felt a glimmer of hope begin to spark inside me. Then, the moon hid itself behind a cloud, and all was darkness only, profound, cold, isolation. Ice-o-lation.

Tears poured down my face, the only source of warmth I could perceive before they chilled and froze, falling ice crystals onto the mound of snow on which I lay. Then I heard someone weeping in the darkness. I wondered if it was myself, but it was not me bawling. I did not make a sound. Another such as I lay alone and freezing very close by.

I did not call out to the other person lost in the dark. I could not speak. I could not move. I could only rest and feel the cold slowly seeping the life away from my deadening body. Another suffered such as I did, and I could not help.

Then I heard a voice shouting out to the crying person. The voice made its way closer to the weeping, and the sounds became one. The shouting shifted into a calm voice, soothing the lost traveler. It comforted the person in the dark.

The man would build a fire, and everything would be okay. There would be warmth again soon. Only a little longer, and everything would be okay. Only a little longer while he ignited the bundle of wood he'd carried with him on his search for her.

I lay there listening to the voice. Somehow, I felt comforted too, even though I knew that no one would come looking for me with a bundle of wood to make a fire and warm me up again.

Although I knew that they were so very close, I could not call out for the help I needed. And would I have called if I could, to these people who were strangers? Would I have interfered at such an intimate moment of friendship between two people I did not know in order to beg assistance for myself?

I could not, in any case, and so the answer doesn't matter. Only I could, and did, find a measure of peace in knowing that another could be in the same situation as I, and that someone could care enough to help.

I expected then I could die with that small measure of peace. I could close my eyes and let the cold take me in this dark, forgotten space, near two people, and therefore *not* alone even if they didn't know I was here.

But then a spark lit up the darkness, and I could see the people. I could see the firelight flickering.

The snow had stopped falling, and the wind blew in a breeze rather than a gale.

The man held the woman and spoke soothing words to her.

The fire blazed up and radiated such warmth that even I could feel its heat where I was. I could feel its warmth! I had thought it impossible to feel anything anymore. I lay there, still obscured from their view, shadowed by the tree, protected by its strong trunk and branches, hidden from these people, and yet slowly warmed by them. The warmth from the fire began to thaw my frozen body, and the warmth of their friendship thawed my heart.